haruko / love poems

June Jordan

haruko / love poems

SERPENT'S TAIL

HIGH RISK BOOKS

NEW YORK / LONDON

The poems in Part II have been previously published in *Passion* (Beacon Press, 1980), *Things That I Do in the Dark* (Beacon Press, 1980), *Living Room* (Thunder's Mouth Press, 1985), and *Naming Our Destiny* (Thunder's Mouth Press, 1980).

First published in the United Kingdom 1993 by
Virago Press Ltd. 20–23 Mandela St., Camden Town, London NW1 0HQ

First U.S. edition published 1994 by
High Risk Books/Serpent's Tail
4 Blackstock Mews, London, England N4 2BT
180 Varick Street, 10th Floor, New York, NY 10014

Library of Congress Cataloging-in-Publication Data

Jordan, June, 1936–
        Haruko : Love poems / June Jordan. — 1st U. S. ed.
            p.   cm.
        ISBN 1-85242-323-4
        1. Love poetry, American.   2. Lesbians—Poetry.   I. Title.
        PS3560.O73H37   1994   93-32425
        811'.54—dc20   CIP

British Library Cataloguing-in-Publication Data

        Jordan, June.
        Haruko/Love Poetry: new and selected Love poems. — (High Risk)
        I. Title   II. Series

Book and cover design by Rex Ray
Printed in Hong Kong by Colorcraft, Ltd.

10   9   8   7   6   5   4   3

Special Acknowledgments

Behind this manuscript of love poems,
this manuscript compiled and completed
when I could not, by myself, do many
things, is a story of great love:

Thanks forever
to Sara Miles and Adrienne Rich
who
fierce, dauntless, and wise
pulled it all together

Thanks to Pratibha Parmar
who flew all the way from London

Thanks to Amy Scholder
who called and came across the Bay

Thanks to Jan Heller Levi
who never lost a single
poem

Thanks to every lover
for the everlasting mystery

dedicated to love

Contents

Foreword

WHAT IS THIS thing called love, in the poems of June Jordan, artist, teacher, social critic, visionary of human solidarity? First of all, it's a motive; the power Che Guevara was trying to invoke in his much-quoted assertion: "At the risk of appearing ridiculous . . . the true revolutionary is moved by great feelings of love." I think also of Paul Nizan: "You think you are innocent if you say, 'I love this woman and I want to act in accordance with my love,' but you are beginning the revolution. . . . You will be driven back: to claim the right to a human act is to attack the forces responsible for all the misery in the world." Neither of them, admittedly, was claiming the love of a woman for women, the love of a man for men, as revolutionary, as a human act.

But the motive is "directed by desire" in Jordan's poetry, and desire is personal, concrete, particular and sensual:

late afternoon and the air
dissolves to luminous and elongated
molecules
a heartfelt mercury as delicate

as compelling
as the melted movements
of your lips

———————

And if I
if I ever let love go
because the hatred and the whispering
became a phantom dictate I o-
bey in lieu of impulse and realities
(the blossoming flamingos of my
wild mimosa trees)
then let love freeze me
out.

I must become
I must become a menace to my enemies.

We are left with the question, Why should feelings
of love appear politically ridiculous, why would we
ever assume that private love can have no public
meaning, or must inevitably be "driven back"? June
Jordan's love poems make clear that fragmentation and
self-denial are impediments both to love and to revo-
lutionary life. In the series of "Haruko Poems" open-
ing this book, a lover gazes into the rejection she is
suffering and refuses it, refuses personal humiliation,
uses the lens of her anger, eroticism, and wit to scrutinize
self-hatred, illumine self-respect, and recruit a mutual
dignity from the failures of mutual desire:

So do we finally recover side by side
what we have loved enough to keep
in spite of passion or love's sorrow.

In the "Selected Love Poems"—written over twenty-two years—Jordan explores many kinds of love, toward herself and others, male and female, always within a context of trying to bridge "apparent differences of turf," whether of gender or race, of time or place, or of pieces of the self. Former lovers can become allies; the connections between desire and solidarity become palpable in many of these poems.

June Jordan is one of the most musically and lyrically gifted poets of the late twentieth century. Her extraordinarily tonal, sensuous poems capture moments or ways of being which might make love—in many dimensions—more possible, more revolution-directed. These reflections on love reach through and out beyond the personal encounter toward a meaning perhaps best enclosed in the last poem in this book:

I am a stranger
learning to worship the strangers
around me

whoever you are
whoever I may become

Adrienne Rich
June 1993

I
Poems For
Haruko
1991–1992

New Year
for Haruko

Here comes the dragon!
Here comes the dog!
Here comes the monkey!
Here comes the apple tree!
Here come the apples!
Here come the acolytes!
Here comes the church!
Here come the shoes!
Here comes the drum!
Here comes the rain!
Here come the blues!
Here comes the shark!
Here comes the head!
Here comes the tail!
Here come dumplings in a little tin pail!
Here comes the snow!
Here come the cows!
Here come the clowns!
Here comes the hill!
Here comes the pearl!
Here come the waves!
Here comes the bread!
Here comes the call!

Here comes the dragon!
Here comes the dog!
Here come the apples!

Here come the acolytes!
Here comes the church!
Here come the shoes!

For Haruko

Little moves on sight
blinded by histories
as trivial or expansive
as the rain
seducing light
into a blurred excitement

Then
she opens
all of one eye
as accurate as longing
as two hands beholden to the hunger
   of green leaves

and
rinsing them back
into regular breath
she who sees
she frees each of these
beggarly events
cleansing them
of dust and other death

Poem for Haruko

I never thought I'd keep a record of my pain
or happiness
like candles lighting the entire soft lace
of the air
around the full length of your hair/a shower
organized by God
in brown and auburn
undulations luminous like particles
of flame

But now I do
retrieve an afternoon of apricots
and water interspersed with cigarettes
and sand and rocks
we walked across:
        How easily you held
my hand
beside the low tide
of the world

Now I do
relive an evening of retreat
a bridge I left behind
where all the solid heat
of lust and tender trembling
lay as cruel and as kind
as passion spins its infinite

4

tergiversations in between the bitter
and the sweet

Alone and longing for you
now I do

12:01 A.M.
for Haruko

I

Rushing like white
waters rapid toward precipitous
and killer rocks
the blood of time alone
escapes control and leaking
useless
dries and quantifies
the liquid loss of impulse
purified by any of your fingertips
that touch my face

6

II

The rain does not become a clock
does not become the rain

III

Thinking about chocolate
I woke up
and tried to move
but where you kept me
nipples and the milk

of mystery bestirred the mouth
of my imagination

IV

Forget about fever
Forget about healthy or unhealthy
this or that
At times
the flesh below the thin skin
of your naked leg
seems to my pilgrim lips
a living column smooth but swollen
with the juice of my new
destiny

V

Then how should I
subsist
without the benediction of our bodies
intertwined
or why?

VI

Somebody else might think I mean
the epiderm the tissues
and the cells
that matter into tangible configurations
only

VII

I am my soul adrift
the whole night sky denies me light
without you

Why I became a pacifist
and then
How I became a warrior again:

Because nothing I could do or say
turned out okay
I figured I should just sit
still and chill
except to maybe mumble
'Baby, Baby:
Stop!'
AND
Because turning that other cheek
    holding my tongue
    refusing to retaliate when the deal
    got ugly
And because not throwing whoever calls me *bitch*
    out the goddamn window
And because swallowing my pride
    saying I'm sorry when whoever don't like
    one single thing
    about me and don't never take a break from
    counting up the 65,899 ways I talk wrong
    I act wrong
And because sitting on my fist
    neglecting to enumerate every incoherent
    rigid/raggedy-ass/disrespectful/killer cold
    and self-infatuated crime against love
    committed by some loudmouth don't know
    nothing about it takes 2 to fuck and
    it takes 2 to fuck things up

And because making apologies that nobody give a shit
    about

and because failing to sing my song

finally
finally

    got on my absolute last nerve

I pick up my sword
I lift up my shield
And I stay ready for war
Because now I live ready for a whole lot more

than that

'CLEAN!'
you spelled out: 'Make it '/'Break it
clean!'
But you meant <u>mean</u>
as in

    <u>mean</u>
    <u>hard</u>
    <u>gone</u>

like how you done me
          <u>mean</u>
          <u>hard</u>
          <u>gone</u>
          <u>hard</u>

          <u>done</u>

Update
for Haruko

More than two months since a carousel of misery
accursed and violent ensnared my mind and
spinning me vertiginous in solitude and
alternating trustful lust with lyrical delirium
or pain irregular as drought or rain
crushed out the flowering of surprise and still today
    drains
all the colors of the world into the pointless
pulverizing dry bed of a dried up hand

So I arrive a neophyte to unconditional
and passionate but passive vigil undercut
by flares of anger or despair that at the last
subside to core forbidden appetite for cigarettes or food
especially Chinese to take out/not too spicy
hot but what I need means hot and shrimp fried
rice becomes three boxed up coals of fire
I hold as close as possible against this wistful skin
this frozen covering for all my love

Still I am learning unconditional and true
Still I am burning unconditional for you

**Poem About Process
And Progress
*for Haruko***

Hey Baby you betta
hurry it up!
Because
since you went totally
off
I seen a full moon
I seen a half moon
I seen a quarter moon
I seen no moon whatsoever!

I seen a equinox
I seen a solstice
I seen Mars and Venus on a line
I seen a mess a fickle stars
and lately
I seen this new kind a luva
on an' off the telephone
who like to talk to me
all the time

real nice

Resolution # 1,003

I will love who loves me
I will love as much as I am loved
I will hate who hates me
I will feel nothing for everyone oblivious to me
I will stay indifferent to indifference
I will live hostile to hostility
I will make myself a passionate and eager lover
   in response to passionate and eager love

I will be nobody's fool

A Poem For
Haruko 10/29

because
it's about my anger
smouldering
because your stillness
kills simplicity
and chills
this willing ardor
swept back
into realms of doubt
and ordinary feats
of regular and unimpassioned
sensible retreat
wherein an ending to my love
for you
will stretch its scaly
full length into light
that shrivels
innocence
and warps the silent mouth
of adoration
into bitten
blighted
bloom
Oh! If you would only walk
into this room
again and touch me anywhere
I swear

I would not long for heaven or
for earth
more than I'd wish to stay there
touched
and touching you

Admittedly
I do not forget
the beauty of one braid
black silk that fell
as loose as it fell long
and everlasting as the twilight
anywhere

Boats afloat
Kayaks capsizing
A skyhawk falling asleep
Wind chimes murmuring into the atmosphere
and high above this peaceful
house
a 90 year old willow tree
sucks on the sunlight
with a thousand toothless leaves
and what do I care
if I never will hear your fast
words slurring
near to my eager ears
again

Taiko Dojo
Messages from Haruko

No! No!
No. No. No. No.
No! No!
No. No. No. No.
No-No-No-No/No-No-No-No/No-No-No-No
No-No-No-No
No! No!
No. No. No. No.
No! No!
No. No. No. No.
No-No-No-No/No-No-No-No
No-No-No-No
No! No!
No-No-No-No
No! No!

NO!

Poem About Heartbreak That
Go On and On

bad love last like a big
ugly lizard crawl around the house
forever
never die
and never change itself

into a butterfly

Speculations on the Present
Through the Prism of the Past
for Haruko

At 29
I climbed on a motorcycle
for my first date
with this guy in front of me
my arms around his waist
as tight as my excitement
my chin nestling on a soft spot
in between his shoulder blades

Zoom!
We just took off:
French bread
and a bottle of French wine
my keys
him and me and the bike

We left
after he said, 'This—'
(meaning my house/my life)
'is just impossible! It's just too
bare! Too poor!'
And so he carried me and the bike
into the unfamiliar darkness of his opulence his city his
apartment his gigantic bed/he
locked me up/he
kept me well fed/absolutely

clean
and (in general) well satisfied
on the sexual side
but scared to say anything
about the 25 foot leather whip
memento from his military duties
in Algiers
that he uncoiled from time
to time
nostalgic

Through the routine eucalyptus fragrance of his
   rooms
Through the river-view windows of his paradise
I watched for tail-light jewels on a nearby evening
   bridge

And I supposed that something
beautiful
might be waiting for me not
too far away
but definitely not
on this side/definitely not
on my side
of the water

Poem for Haruko

All day I did things fast
picking up leaves
scrubbing a saucepan clean
racing through an Asian American anthology
of poems
All because it hurt so much
to think about you hurt
because
I moved so slowly
and in circles
seemingly insensible
to how you held a towel
wide as your slender arms are long
to fold around me
shivering from the bathtub
how you held a children's story
close to my almost closing eyelids
how you held me
free
as I could ever hope
to be

Ichiban

Good bye.

> I do not choose
> to collaborate
> and lose
> the golden blues' delirium
> in this and that
> cynical or reckless
> rat-a-tat tat-tat-tat
> chit-chat
>
> ICHIBAN

Good bye.

> I take back my
> body tractable and loaded up for bliss
> I take back my
> mind become inebriate and apostolic to
>   desire
> I take back my
> heart beating to the intimations of your lips
> I take back my
> spirit riveted in fire
>
> ICHIBAN

Good bye.

Phoenix Mystery # 1

The thing about fire
is every kind of moving
light
but the fever that enflames
the blood
ignites the air itself
between two stones
and lifts the world
into a crackling and molecular display
as complicated and seductive
as apocalypse
or else the baited/risen breath
surrendering to the deep
insistence
of uncommon
sexual bliss

The thing about fire
is not unlike all tragedy
that leads you to the house
and takes your hat
your coat
your shoes
and then begins a simmering
destruction of the floor the walls
the ceilings and the door
become a crematorium

a furnace burying the sky
beyond
a mountainous volcanic cloud consumes
the oxygen the photographs
of daily life eternal
as the lover
who survives to search the ashes
for what's hot
a bone chip charred
but irreducible among the burning ruins

Phoenix Mystery # 2
for Haruko

The thing about fire
is
ashes in a supermarket
paper bag
but then
you see smoke
rising hot
and serious (and imperious)
again

Postscript for Haruko:
On War and Peace

How still these oak and maple trees stand
side by side in slowly melting snow
Not one attacks or seeks incineration
for the other. Not even mysteries of birds
that missed the last sure flight to safety
interject disturbance of this winter
night when patience seems as natural
as the cold air holding all that's there
serene and lifted by a star's light
as specific in its glitter as it's far.

So do we finally outlive the flare and flash
of flame and leaf and feathers violent
as waves that rise because they also fall
away and falling call the waters of the world
one name again.

So do we finally recover side by side
what we have loved enough to keep
in spite of passion or love's sorrow.

'Haruko:
Oh! It's like <u>stringbean</u> in French?'

'No:
It's like <u>hurricane</u>
in English!'

Big City Happening
for Haruko

Try exquisite in the New York concept
   of these tracks
below the subway
platform
far below the sidewalk
concrete
perforated/tricky
mica fireworks
that scatter microscopic
on the almost rising surface
of the street

And I do.
I ride these tracks to meet you:
moving through/an upright register
of shadow and of light
moving through
eclectic ganglia of open cities/nervous
nowhere immaculate nowhere a mystery
to match this urban earthquake travelling
stop by stop
into reunion
with the highway wonder
of your eyes

**Poem on the
Quantum Mechanics of
Breakfast with Haruko**

Sutter and Stockton/one block North of Union
    Square
less than a week ago
seemed simple to me/we
were there

And easy as that San Francisco morning
you ate
memories of Paris
from a plate of sliced papaya
thick
buttered toast
and sent strong current
sidelong glances
towards the handsome white man
(white shirt/no tie)
sitting
possibly oblivious
behind you

One block north of Union Square
but what is union
anyway
or union squared
or North

as I am flying East to London
now
above the secrets of the raw
intractable
blue waters of the blue
Atlantic

and I still stay
willing inches away from your hand
almost too small
to lift the thick
crisp
buttered toast
into the not quite neutral
air
between us

Mendocino Memory
for Haruko

Half moon
cold and low above the poplar tree
and sweet pea petals
pink and white/what
happened
on this personal best night
for casual stars
and silky constellations
streaming brilliant
through the far
forgetful darkness
of the sky

I found the other half
above the pillow
where you lay
asleep
face to one side
with nothing in this world
or the next
to hide

Letter to Haruko
From Decorah, Iowa, USA

In this white space this American
page of immigration from three months
of darkness in Norway/hunger
unrelieved by sun or flowerlight
or playful ambulations through an easy
day
I stand beside a stranger
ice and snow stretched pale for miles
behind me
village streets bare/no
trees/pedestrians/dogs/or shadow
on the hard brick of the local
will to presevere
to stay until the whisperings of spring arrive
to marry
to bake bread
to break a window out of solid log
cabin walls that wheeze with winter
inescapable

A stranger points to handicrafts
traditional
in hand-hewn pine and homemade paints
that sanctify a bed a chair a bowl
with hours of devotion
agitant against a loneliness as unmistakable
as thirst or sex

and I am taken by these florid
refutations of a frozen near horizon
brilliant tokens of a flesh soft loom that held
some woman's sanity together
ravelling intelligence
like thread that magical
became a cloth
of loving color

And I am straining to converge
this plain
midwestern/fasting stand of oak trees
quiet as they ramify
in such thin air
with your true
handheld miracles of rain
your expert
California camera capturing
a lush a sudden deluge
from an otherwise
dry sky

But the roots
for a connection that can keep
Japan and San Francisco
and Jamaica and Decorah
Iowa and Norway
all in one place palpable
to any sweet belief
move deep below
apparent differences of turf

I trace them in the lifeline
of an open palm
a hand that works
its homemade heat
against the jealous
hibernating blindness
of the night

plum blossom plum jam
even the tree becomes something
more than a skeleton
longing for the sky

II
Selected Love
Poems
1970–1991

Roman Poem Number Thirteen
for Eddie

Only our hearts will argue hard
against the small lights letting in the news
and who can choose between the worst possibility
and the last
between the winners of the wars against the breathing
and the last
war everyone will lose
and who can choose between the dry gas
domination of the future
and the past
between the consequences of the killers
and the past
of all the killing? There
is no choice in these.
Your voice
breaks very close to me my love.

40

Roman Poem Number Fourteen

believe it love
believe

     my lover
lying down he
lifts me up and high
and I am
high on him

believe it love
believe

the carnage scores around
the corner

o believe it love
believe

the bleeding fills the carnage cup
my lover lifts me
I am up
     and love is lying down

believe
believe it

crazies wear a clean shirt to the fire

o my lover
lift me higher higher

crazies take a scream and
make a speech they talk and
wash their mouths in dirt
no love will hurt
me lover lift me lying down

believe
believe it
carnage crazies
snap smash more more
(what you waiting for?)

you own the rope knife rifles the whole list
the searing bomb starch brighteners
the nuclear family whiteners

look the bridge be fallen down
look the ashes from the bones turn brown
look the mushroom hides the town
look the general wears his drip dry red
drip gown

o my lover nakedly
believe my love

believe
believe it

Onesided Dialog

OK. So she got back the baby
but what happened to the record player?

No shit. The authorized appropriation
contradicts my falling out of love?

You're wrong. It's not that I gave away my keys.
The problem is nobody wants to steal me or my
  house.

Poem for My Pretty Man

the complexity is like your legs
around me
simple
an entanglement
and strong
the ready
curling
hair
the brownskin tones of action
quiet
temporarily
like listening
serene
and passionate
and
slowly closer
slowly
closer
kissing

inch by inch

From the Talking Back of Miss Valentine Jones: Poem # One

well I wanted to braid my hair
bathe and bedeck my
self so fine
so fully aforethought for
your pleasure
see:
I wanted to travel and read
and runaround fantastic
into war and peace:
I wanted to
surf
dive
fly
climb
conquer
and be conquered
THEN
I wanted to pickup the phone
and find you asking me
if I might possibly be alone
some night
(so I could answer cool
as the jewels I would wear
on bareskin for your
digmedaddy delectation:)
'WHEN
you coming ova?'

But
I had to remember to write down
margarine on the list
and shoepolish and a can of
sliced pineapples in casea company
and a quarta skim milk cause Teresa's
gainin weight and don' nobody groove on
that much
girl
and next I hadta sort for darks and lights before
the laundry hit the water which I had
to kinda keep a eye on be-
cause if the big hose jumps the sink again that
Mrs. Thompson gointa come upstairs
and brain me with a mop don' smell too
nice even though she hang
it headfirst out the winda
and I had to check
on William like to
burn hisself to death with fever
boy so thin be
calling all day 'Momma! Sing to me?'
'Ma! Am I gone die?' and me not
wake enough to sit beside him longer than
to wipeaway the sweat or change the sheets/
his shirt and feed him orange
juice before I fall out sleep and
Sweet My Jesus ain but one can
left
and we not thru the afternoon

and now
you (temporarily) shown up with a thing
you say's a poem and you
call it
'Will The Real Miss Black America Stand Up?'

> guilty po' mouth
> about duty beauties of my
> headrag
> boozedup doozies about
> never mind
> cause love is blind

well
I can't use it

and the very next bodacious Blackman
call me queen
because my life ain shit
because (in any case) he ain been here to share it
with me
(dish for dish and do for do and
dream for dream)
I'm gone scream him out my house
be-
cause what I wanted was
to braid my hair/bathe and bedeck my
self so fully be-
cause what I wanted was
your love
not pity

be-
cause what I wanted was
your love
your love

For Christopher

Tonight
　　the machinery of shadow
　　　moves into the light

He is lying there
　　not a true invalid
　　　　not dying

Now his face looks blue
　　but all of that small body
　　　will more than do
　　　　　as life.

The lady radiologist
　　　　regardless how and where
　　　　　she turns the knob

will never know
　　　the plenty of pain
　　　　　　growing

parts to arm
　　a man inside the boy

practically asleep

A Sonnet for A.B.T.

But one of these Wednesdays everything could work
the phone and the answering machine: Your voice
despite the 65 miles that would irk
or exhaust a fainthearted lover: Your choice
of this distance this timing between us bends
things around: Illusory landmarks of longing and
    speed.
A full moon the light of summer sends
to light a branch the leaves no longer need.

A top ten lyric fallen to eleven
But meaningful (*meaningful*) because the music still
invites a kind of close tight heaven
of a slowdown dance to let me kill the chill.

You know what I mean
My Love: Seen or unseen

The Wedding

Tyrone married her this afternoon
not smiling as he took the aisle
and her slightly rough hand.
Dizzella listened to the minister
staring at his wrist and twice
forgetting her name:
Do you promise to obey?
Will you honor humility and love
as poor as you are?
Tyrone stood small but next
to her person
trembling. Tyrone stood
straight and bony
black alone with one key
in his pocket
By marrying today
they made themselves a man
and woman
answered friends or unknown
curious about the Cadillacs
displayed in front of Beaulah Baptist.
Beaulah Baptist
life in general
indifferent
barely known
nor caring to consider
the earlywed Tyrone
and his Dizzella

brave enough
but only two.

The Reception

Doretha wore the short blue lace last night
and William watched her drinking so she fight
with him in flying collar slim-jim orange
tie and alligator belt below the navel pants uptight

'I flirt. You hear me? Yes I flirt.
Been on my pretty knees all week
to clean the rich white downtown dirt
the greedy garbage money reek.

I flirt. Damned right. You look at me.'
But William watched her carefully
his mustache shaky she could see
him jealous, 'which is how he always be

at parties.' Clementine and Wilhelmina
looked at trouble in the light blue lace
and held to George while Roosevelt Senior
circled by the yella high and bitterly light blue face

He liked because she worked
the crowded room like clay like molding men
from dust to muscle jerked
the arms and shoulders moving when
she moved.

The Lord Almighty Seagrams
bless

Doretha in her short blue dress
and Roosevelt waiting for his chance:
a true gut-funky blues to make her really dance.

Poem for My Love

How do we come to be here next to each other
in the night
Where are the stars that show us to our love
inevitable
Outside the leaves flame usual in darkness
and the rain
falls cool and blessed on the holy flesh
the black men waiting on the corner for
a womanly mirage
I am amazed by peace
It is this possibility of you
asleep
and breathing in the quiet air

Poem for Joy
Dedicated to the Creek Tribe of North America

Dreaming
    Colorado where the whole earth rises
    marvellous high hard rock higher than
       the heart can
    calmly tolerate: the hawk
    swoons from its fierce precipitation
    granite in its rising opposition to the bird
    or rabbit
    Sapling leaf or stallion loose among the chasmic
    crevices dividing continental
    stretch into the small scale appetizers
    then the lifted meal
    itself

And dazed
    by snowlight settled like a glossary
    of diamonds on the difficult
    ice-bitten mountain trails that lead
    to fish rich waters

I reach
    the birthplace for the stories of your hurt
    your soft collapse
    the feelings of the flat wound of the not
       forgotten graves

where neither rain nor dawn
can resurrect the stolen pageantry the blister

details of the taken acreage
that scars two million memories of forest
blueberry bush and sudden
mushrooms sharing dirt
with footprints tender as the hesitations
of your hand
                who know obliteration
                who arise from the abyss
                the aboriginal
                as definite as heated through as dry
                around the eyes
                as Arizona
                the aboriginal
                as apparently inclement as invincible
                as porous
                as the desert
                the aboriginal
                from whom the mountains slide
                away
                afraid to block the day's deliverance
                into stars and cool air lonely
                for the infinite invention of avenging
                    fires

And now the wolf
And now the loyalty of wolves
And now the bear
And now the vast amusement of the bears

And now the aboriginal
And now the daughter of the tomb.

And now an only child of the dead becomes the
    mother
of another life,
And how shall the living sing of that
impossibility?
        She will.

Ghazal at Full Moon

I try to describe how this aching begins or how it
began
with an obsolete coin and the obsolete head of an
obsolete Indian.

Holding a nickel I beheld a buffalo I beheld the silver
face
of a man who might be your father: A dead man: An
Indian.

I thought, 'Indians pray. Indians dance. But, mostly,
Indians do not live.'
In the U.S.A., we said, 'The only good Indian is a
dead Indian.'

Dumb like Christopher Columbus I could not factor
out the obvious
denominator: Guatemala/Wisconsin/Jamaica/
Colorado:
Indian

Nicaragua and Brazil, Arizona, Illinois, North Dakota
and New Mexico:
The Indigenous: The shining and the shadow of the
eye is Indian.

One billion-fifty-six, five-hundred-and-thirty-seven-
thousand people

breathing in India, Pakistan, Bangladesh: All of them
Indian.

Ocho Ríos Oklahoma Las Vegas Pearl Lagoon
Chicago
Bombay Panjim Liverpool Lahore Comalapa
Glasgow:
Indian.

From a London pub among the lager louts to Macchu
Picchu
I am following an irresistible a tenuous and livid
profile: Indian

I find a surging latticework inside the merciless
detritus
of diaspora
We go from death to death who see any difference
here
from Indian.

The voice desiring your tongue transmits from the
light of the clouds as it can.
Indian Indian Indian   Indian Indian Indian Indian.

Poem Number Two on
Bell's Theorem
or The New Physicality of Long Distance Love

There is no chance that we will fall apart
There is no chance
There are no parts.

Leaves Blow Backward

leaves blow backward with the wind
behind them beautiful
and almost run through atmosphere
of flying birds
or butterflies turn light
more freely than my mouth
learns to kiss by speaking
among aliens.

Romance in Irony

        I would risk ticks
and Rocky Mountain Spotted Fever
stop smoking
give up the car and the VCR
destabilize my bank account
floss before as well as after meals
and unilaterally disarm my telephone connection

                                                           to

other (possible) lovers
if
we could walk into the mountains then
come home again
together

But instead
I lie in bed
fingering photographs from Colorado
that conceal more than they illuminate
the hunter of the elksong or the deer.

I resent the radiator heat
that nightly rises almost musical
in a wet hot air
crescendo
or I exaggerate some not bad looking trees
that 2 or maybe 3 feet there (away from me)

and out the window
grow
oblivious above a miscellaneous
debris
(I yearn for non-negotiable abutment
to the beauty of the world)

And with the courage that the lonely or the
                foolish keep
I set the clock
turn out the light
and do not dream and do not sleep

Roman Poem Number Nine

Return is not a way of going forward
after all
or back. In any case it seems
a matter of opinion how
you face although
the changing bed the different voice
around the different room

may testify to movement
entry exit it
is motion takes you in
and memory that lets you out again.
Or
as this love will let me say
the body travels faster than the keeping
heart will turn away.

x

Roman Poem Number Ten

Quarter past midnight and the sea
the dark blue music
does not belong to me

an elephant desire
heavy speeding whisper phantom
elephantom atmosphere

the heart rip hurts me
like the let go at the cliff

fell down shallow
loose and cold

let go
let go

About the Reunion

'I am rarely vindictive but
this summer I have taken great
pleasure in killing mosquitoes'

He says that to me
It is quite dark where we sit
and difficult to see

or tells me of work he will do
films of no end no beginning
and pours more wine
or takes another cigarette

And I know that is probably true
of his life of our love not to begin
not to end not be ugly or fine

But there is this history of once
when his hands and the length of his legs
came suddenly
to claim me all
bone and all flesh forcing away
the wall and the image of the wall
in one
fast meeting of amazement

And that was another year and somewhere
else

Here we talk outside
or do not talk
almost asleep in separated
wood chairs as hard as the time
between us
and
I admit
you are not as tall as the trees around me
your eyes are not as open as surprising
as the sea

but I watch for your words any changing
of your head

from a deadspot in the darkness
to a face

and finally you move

'I have to get in touch with
some other people'
you say
after so much silence

and I do not move

and
you leave.

Poem for Mark

England, I thought, will look like Africa
or India with elephants and pale men
pushing things about
rifle and gloves
handlebar mustache and tea
pith helmets
riding crop
The Holy Bible
and a rolled up map of plunder
possibilities

But schoolboys with schoolbags
little enough for sweets
more Wellingtons into the manicured
mud
and Cockney manners
('I say
we've been waiting 45 minutes
for this bus, we 'ave! It's
a regular disgrace,
it 'tis!'
'Yes, love: I'm sorry! But
step up/move along,
now! I'm doing the best I can!
You can
write a letter if you please!')
quite outclassed the Queen's

And time felt like a flag
right side up and flying
high while mousse-spike haircuts
denim jackets strolled around
and Afro-Caribbean/Afro-Celtic men
and women comfortable in full
length Rasta dreads
invited me to dinner or
presented me with poetry
And we
sat opposite but close
debating Nicaragua
or the civil liberties of countries

under siege
and you said
'Rubbish!' to the notion of a national
identity
and if I answered,
'In my country—'
You would interrupt me, saying,
'You're not serious!'
but then I thought I was
about 'my country'
meaning where I'd come from
recently
and after only transatlantic static for a single
phone call
up against my loathing to disrupt and travel
to the silly land of Philip and Diana
never having hoped for anyone (a bebop-

antelope) like you
so quietly impertinent and teasing
it was 4 a.m. the first time
when we stopped the conversation
And long before my face lay nestling on the hotel
pillows/well
I knew
whoever the hell 'my people'
are
I knew that one of them
is you

In Memoriam
Poem for Mrs. Fannie Lou Hamer

You used to say, 'June?
Honey when you come down here you
supposed to stay with me. Where
else?'
Meanin home
against the beer the shotguns and the
point of view of whitemen don'
never see Black anybodies without
some violent itch start up.
                              The ones who
said, 'No Nigga's Votin in This Town . . .

less'n it be feet first to the booth'
Then jailed you
beat you brutal
bloody/battered/beat
you blue beyond the feeling
of the terrible

And failed to stop you.
Only God could but He
wouldn't stop
you
fortress from self-
pity
Humble as a woman anywhere
I remember finding you inside the

laundromat
in Ruleville
<blockquote>

lion spine relaxed/hell
what's the point to courage
when you washin clothes?
</blockquote>

But that took courage

<blockquote>

just to sit there/target
to the killers lookin
for your singin face
perspirey through the rinse
and spin
</blockquote>

and later
you stood mighty in the door on James Street
loud callin:

<blockquote>

'BULLETS OR NO BULLETS!
THE FOOD IS COOKED
AN' GETTIN COLD!'
</blockquote>

We ate
A family tremulous but fortified
by turnips/okra/handpicked
like the lilies

filled to the very living
full
one solid gospel
(sanctified)

one gospel

(peace)

one full Black lily
luminescent
in a homemade field

of love

West Coast Episode

Eddie hung a light globe with the best electric
tape
he could find in
five minutes

then he left the room where he lives
to meet me
        (in Los Angeles)
Meanwhile the light globe fell and
smashed glass everywhere
        (the waterbed
        was dangerous
        for days)
but we used the paperbag that hid
the dollar-twenty-nine-California-Champagne
to hide
the light bulb
with a warm brown atmosphere

and that
worked really well

so there was no problem
except
we had to walk like feet
on broken seashells
even though

the color of the rug was green
and out beyond the one room
of our love
the world was mostly
dry.

It's About You: On the Beach

You have
two hands absolutely lean and clean
to let go the gold
the silver flat or plain rock
sand
but hold the purple pieces
atom articles
that glorify a color
yours is orange
oranges are like you love
a promising
a calm skin and a juice
inside
a juice
a running from the desert
Lord
see how you run
YOUR BODY IS A LONG BLACK WING
YOUR BODY IS A LONG BLACK WING

Of Nightsong and Flight

There are things lovely and dangerous still

the rain
when the heat of an evening
sweetens the darkness with mist

and the eyes cannot see what the memory will
of new pain

when the headlights deceive
like the windows wild birds believe to be air
and bash bodies and wings
on the glass

when the headlights show space
but the house and the room and the bed and your face
are still there

while I am mistaken
and try to drive by

the actual kiss
of the world everywhere

After All Is Said and Done

Maybe you thought I would forget
about the sunrise
how the moon stayed in the morning
time a lower lip
your partly open partly spoken
mouth

Maybe you thought I would exaggerate
the fire of the stars
the fire of the wet wood burning by
the waterside
the fire of the fuck the sudden move
you made me make
to meet you
(fire)

BABY
I do not exaggerate and
if
I could
I would.

On My Happy/Matrimonial Condition

last time I got married was
yesterday (in
bed)
we stayed there
talking it over
nobody
shook
hands
but
the agreement
felt
very good
as a matter of fact
so
that was what
will be
the absolute
last time I ever
get
married

No Poem Because
Time Is Not a Name

But beyond the
anxiety
the
querulous and reckless intersecting
conflict
and the trivial misleading banal
and separating fences every scrim
disguise each mask and feint
red herrings broadside poor
maneuvers of the
begging
hopeful
heart that wants and waits the
head that works against the minute
minute
There are pictures/memories of
temperature or cast or tone
or hue and vision
pictures of a dream
and dreams of memories and
dreams of gardens dreams of film
and pictures
of the daring
simple
fabulous
bold
difficult

and distant
inextricable
main
nigger
that I love
and
this is not
a poem

On a New Year's Eve

Infinity doesn't interest me

not altogether
anymore

I crawl and kneel and grub about
I beg and listen for

what can go away

            (as easily as love)

or perish
like the children
running
hard on oneway streets/infinity
doesn't interest me

not anymore

not even
repetition your/my/eye-
lid or the colorings of sunrise
or all the sky excitement
added up

is not enough

to satisfy this lusting adulation that I feel
for
your brown arm before it
moves

MOVES
CHANGES UP

the temporary sacred
tales ago
first bikeride round the house
when you first saw a squat
opossum
carry babies on her back

opossum up
in the persimmon tree
you reeling toward
that natural
first
absurdity
with so much wonder still
it shakes your voice

            the temporary is the sacred
            takes me out

and even the stars and even the snow and even
the rain
do not amount to much

unless these things submit to some disturbance
some derangement such
as when I yield myself/belonging
to your unmistaken
body

and let the powerful lock up the canyon/mountain
peaks the
hidden rivers/waterfalls the
deepdown minerals/the coalfields/goldfields/
diamond mines close by the whoring ore
hot
at the center of the earth
spinning fast as numbers
I cannot imagine

let the world blot
obliterate remove so-
called
magnificence
so-called
almighty/fathomless and everlasting
treasures/
wealth
(whatever that may be)

it is this time
that matters

it is this history
I care about

the one we make together
awkward
inconsistent
as a lame cat on the loose
or quick as kids freed by the bell
or else as strictly
once
as only life must mean
a once upon a time
I have rejected propaganda teaching me
about the beautiful
the truly rare

86   (supposedly
the soft push of the ocean at the hushpoint of the shore
supposedly
the soft push of the ocean at the hushpoint of the shore
is beautiful
for instance)
but
the truly rare can stay out there

I have rejected that
abstraction that enormity
unless I see a dog walk on the beach/
a bird seize sandflies
or yourself
approach me
laughing out a sound to spoil
the pretty picture

make an uncontrolled
heartbeating memory
instead

I read the papers preaching on
that oil and oxygen
that redwoods and the evergreens
that trees the waters and the atmosphere
compile a final listing of the world in
short supply

but all alive and all the lives
persist perpetual
in jeopardy
persist
as scarce as every one of us
as difficult to find
or keep
as irreplaceable
as frail
as every one of us

and
as I watch your arm/your
brown arm
just
before it moves

I know

all things are dear
that disappear

all things are dear
that disappear

Sunflower Sonnet
Number One

But if I tell you how my heart swings wide
enough to motivate flirtations with the trees
or how the happiness of passion freaks inside
me, will you then believe the faithful, yearning freeze
on random, fast explosions that I place
upon my lust? Or must I say the streets are bare
unless it is your door I face
unless they are your eyes that, rare
as tulips on a cold night, trick my mind
to oranges and yellow flames around a seed
as deep as anyone may find
in magic? What do you need?

I'll give you that, I hope, and more
But don't you be the one to choose me: poor.

Sunflower Sonnet
Number Two

Supposing we could just go on as two
voracious in the days apart as well as when
we side by side (the many ways we do
that) well! I would consider then
perfection possible, or else worthwhile
to think about. Which is to say
I guess the costs of long term tend to pile
up, block and complicate, erase away
the accidental, temporary, near
thing/pulsebeat promises one makes
because the chance, the easy new, is there
in front of you. But still, perfection takes
some sacrifice of falling stars for rare.
And there are stars, but none of you, to spare.

You Came with Shells

You came with shells. And left them:
shells.
They lay beautiful on the table.
Now they lie on my desk
peculiar
extraordinary under 60 watts.

This morning I disturb I destroy the window
(and its light) by moving my feet
in the water. There.
It's gone.
Last night the moon ranged from the left
to the right side
of the windshield. Only white lines
on a road strike me as
reasonable but
nevertheless and too often
we slow down for the fog.

I was going to say a natural environment
means this or
I was going to say we remain out of our
element or
sometimes you can get away completely
but the shells
will tell about the howling
and the loss

Queen Anne's Lace

Unseemly as a marvelous an astral renegade
now luminous and startling (rakish)
at the top of its thin/ordinary stem
the flower overpowers and outstares me
as I walk by thinking *weeds* and *poison
ivy, bush* and *fern* or *runaway grass:*

You (where are you, really?) never leave me
to my boredom: numb as I might like to be.
Repeatedly
you do revive
arouse alive

a suffering.

Not Looking

Not looking now and then I find you here
not knowing where you are.
Talk to me. Tell me the things I see
fill the table between us or surround
the precipice nobody dares to forget.
Talking takes time takes everything
sooner than I can forget the precipice
and speak to your being there
where I hear you move no nearer
than you were standing on my hands
covered my eyes dreaming about music.

When I or Else

when I or else when you
and I or we
deliberate I lose I
cannot choose if you if
we then near or where
unless I stand as loser
of that losing possibility
that something that I have
or always want more than much
more at
least to have as less and
yes directed by desire

On Your Love

Beloved
where I have been
if
you loved me more than your own
and God's
soul
you could not have lifted me
out of the water
or
lit even one of the cigarettes I stood
smoking alone

Beloved
what I have done
if
you discounted the devil
entirely
and rejected the truth as a rumor
you
would turn from the heat of my face
that burns
under your lips.

Beloved
what I have dreamed
if
you ended the fevers and riot

the claw and the wail and the absolute
furious
dishevel of my unkempt mind
you
could never believe the quiet
your arms
make true around me.

In your love I am sometimes redeemed
a stranger
to myself.

Free Flight

Nothing fills me up at night
I fall asleep for one or two hours then
up again my gut
alarms
I must arise
and wandering into the refrigerator
think about evaporated milk homemade vanilla ice
    cream
cherry pie hot from the oven with Something Like
    Vermont
Cheddar Cheese disintegrating luscious
on the top while
mildly
I devour almonds and raisins mixed to mathematical
criteria or celery or my very own sweet and sour snack
composed of brie peanut butter honey and
a minuscule slice of party size salami
on a single whole wheat cracker no salt added
or I read Cesar Vallejo/Gabriela Mistral/last year's
complete anthology or
I might begin another list of things to do
that starts with toilet paper and
I notice that I never jot down fresh
strawberry shortcake: never
even though fresh strawberry shortcake shoots down
raisins and almonds 6 to nothing
effortlessly

effortlessly
is this poem on my list?
light bulbs lemons envelopes ballpoint refill
post office and zucchini
oranges no
it's not
I guess that means I just forgot
walking my dog around the block leads
to a space in my mind where
during the newspaper strike questions
sizzle through suddenly like
Is there an earthquake down in Ecuador?
Did a TWA supersaver flight to San Francisco
land in Philadelphia instead

or
whatever happened to human rights
In Washington D.C.? Or what about downward
    destabilization
of the consumer price index
and I was in this school P.S. Tum-ta-Tum and time
    came
for me to leave but
No! I couldn't leave: The Rule was anybody leaving
the premises without having taught somebody
    something
valuable would be henceforth proscribed from the
premises would be forever null and void/dull and
vilified well
I had stood in front of 40 to 50 students running my
mouth and I had been generous with deceitful smiles/
    soft-

spoken and pseudo-gentle wiles if and when forced
into discourse amongst such adults as constitutes
the regular treacheries of On The Job Behavior
ON THE JOB BEHAVIOR
is this poem on that list
polish shoes file nails coordinate tops and bottoms
lipstick control no
screaming I'm bored because
this is whoring away the hours of god's creation
pay attention to your eyes your hands the twilight
sky in the institutional big windows
no
I did not presume I was not so bold as to put this
poem on that list
then at the end of the class this boy gives me Mahler's
   9th
symphony the double album listen
to it let it seep into you he
says transcendental love
he says
I think naw
I been angry all day long/nobody did the assignment
I am not prepared
I am not prepared for so much grace
the catapulting music of surprise that makes me
hideaway my face
nothing fills me up at night
yesterday the houseguest left a brown
towel in the bathroom for tonight
I set out a blue one and
an off-white washcloth seriously

I don't need no houseguest
I don't need no towels/lovers
I just need a dog

Maybe I'm kidding.

Maybe I need a woman
a woman be so well you know so wifelike
so more or less motherly so listening so much
the universal skin you love to touch and who the
closer she gets to you the better she looks to me/
    somebody
say yes and make me laugh and tell me she know she
been there she spit bullets at my enemies she say you
need to sail around Alaska fuck it all try this new
cerebral tea and take a long bath

Maybe I need a man
a man be so well you know so manly so lifelike
so more or less virile so sure so much the deep
voice of opinion and the shoulders like a window
seat and cheeks so closely shaven by a twin-edged
razor blade no oily hair and no dandruff besides/
somebody say yes and make
me laugh and tell me he know he been there he spit
bullets at my enemies he say you need to sail around
Alaska fuck it all and take a long bath

lah-ti-dah and lah-ti-dum
what's this socialized obsession with the bathtub

Maybe I just need to love myself myself
(anyhow I'm more familiar with the subject)
Maybe when my cousin tells me you remind me
of a woman past her prime maybe I need
to hustle my cousin into a hammerlock
position make her cry out uncle and
I'm sorry
Maybe when I feel this horrible
inclination to kiss folks I despise
because the party's like that
an occasion to be kissing people
you despise maybe I should tell them kindly
kiss my

Maybe when I wake up in the middle of the night
I should go downstairs
dump the refrigerator contents on the floor
and stand there in the middle of the spilled milk
and the wasted butter spread beneath my dirty feet
writing poems
writing poems
maybe I just need to love myself myself and
anyway
I'm working on it

The snow
　　nearly as soft
　　as the sleeping nipple
　　of your left breast

Inaugural Rose

Wanting to stomp down Eighth Avenue snow
or no snow where you might be so we
can takeover the evening by taxi
by kerosene lamp by literal cups of tea

that you love me

wanting to say, 'Jesus, I'm glad. And I am not
calm: Not calm!' But I
am shy. And shy is short
on reach and wide on bowing
out. It's in:
against the flint and deep
irradiation of this torso listing
to the phosphorescence of French windows in
the bells/your hair/the forehead
of the morning of your face a clear
a calm decision of the light
to gather there

And you an obstinate an elegant
nail-bitten hand on quandaries of self-correction/
self-perfection as political as building your own
bed to tell the truth in
And your waist as narrow as the questions
you insist upon palpate/
expose immense not knowing any of the words
to say *okay* or *wrong*

And my wanting to say
wanting to show and tell *bells/*
okay because I'm shy
but I
will not lie

to you

Poem # 2 for
Inaugural Rose

Calling you from my kitchen to the one where you
   cook
for strangers and it hits me how we fall
into usefulness/change into steak or sausage or
(more frequently) fried chicken
like glut to the gluttonous/choosing a leg a poem
a voice and even a smile a breast/dark or light
   moments
of the mind: how
they throw out the rest or adjudicate the best of
   our
feeling/inedible because somersault singing in silence
will not flake to the fork at 425 or any kind of cue
will not do
and joy is not nice on ice: joy is not nice
But thinking about you over there at the stove
while I sit near the sink and we are not turkey/
I am not ham or bananas/nothing about you
reminds me of money or grist for the fist
and so on and so on but outside you know there is
rain to no purpose in the cockroach concrete of this
common predicament
and I find myself transfixed by the downpour un-
necessarily beating my blood up to the (something
   inside me
wants to say the *visual instinct of your face* or
sometimes I need to write Drums to Overcome the

    Terrors
of Iran but really
it's about the) grace the chimerical
rising of your own and secret eyes to surprise
and to surprise
and to surprise

me

The Morning on the Mountains

The morning on the mountains where the mist
diffuses
down into the depths of the leaves
of the ash and oak trees
trickling toward the complexion of the whole lake
cold
even though the overlooking sky
so solemnly vermilion
sub-divides/the
seething stripes as soft
as sweet as the opening
of your mouth

Toward a City That Sings

Into the topaz the crystalline signals
of Manhattan
the nightplane lowers my body
scintillate with longing to lie positive
beside
the electric waters of your flesh
and
I will never tell you the meaning of this poem:
Just say, 'She wrote it and I recognize
the reference.' Please
let it go at that. Although
it is all the willingness you lend
the world
as when you picked it up
the garbage scattering the cool
formalities of Madison Avenue
after midnight (where we walked
for miles as though we knew the woods
well enough to ignore the darkness)
although it is all the willingness you lend
the world
that makes me want
to clean up everything
in sight
(myself included)

for your possible
discovery

Poem for Nana

What will we do
when there is nobody left
to kill?

■

40,000 gallons of oil gushing into
the ocean
but I
sit on top this mountainside above
the Pacific
checking out the flowers
the California poppies orange
as I meet myself in heat
                    I'm wondering
     where's the Indians?

                    all this filmstrip territory
                    all this cowboy sagaland:
                    not
                    a single Indian
                    in sight

40,000 gallons gushing up poison
from the deepest seabeds
every hour

40,000 gallons
while

experts international
while
new pollutants
swallow the unfathomable
still:

  no indians

I'm staring hard around me
past the pinks the poppies and the precipice
that let me see the wide Pacific
unsuspecting
even trivial
by virtue of its vast surrender

110

I am a woman searching for her savagery
even if it's doomed

Where are the Indians?

■

Crow Nose
Little Bear
Slim Girl
Black Elk
Fox Belly

the people of the sacred trees
and rivers precious to the stars that told
old stories to the night

how do we follow after you?

falling
snow before the firelight
and buffalo as brothers
to the man

how do we follow into that?

■

They found her face down
where she would be dancing
to the shadow drums that humble
birds to silent
       flight

They found her body held
its life dispelled
by ice
my life burns to destroy

Anna Mae Pictou Aquash
slain on the Trail of Broken Treaties
bullet lodged in her brain/hands
and fingertips
dismembered

who won the only peace
that cannot pass
from mouth to mouth

■

Memory should agitate
the pierced bone crack
of one in pushed-back horror
pushed-back pain
as when I call out looking for my face
among the wounded coins
to toss about
or out
entirely
the legends of Geronimo
of Pocahontas
now become a squat
pedestrian cement inside the tomb
of all my trust

as when I feel you isolate
among the hungers of the trees
a trembling
hidden tinder so long unsolicited
by flame

as when I accept my sister dead
when there should be (instead)
a fluid holiness
of spirit wrapped around the world
redeemed by women
whispering communion

■

I find my way by following your spine

Your heart indivisible from my real wish
we
compelled the moon into the evening when
you said, 'No,
I will not let go
of your hand.'

■

Now I am diving for a tide to take me everywhere

Below
the soft Pacific spoils
a purple girdling of the globe
impregnable

■

Last year the South African Minister of Justice
described Anti-Government Disturbances as
Part of a Worldwide Trend toward the
Breakdown of Established Political and Cultural
Orders

■

God knows I hope he's right.

First full moon of a new and final decade
so
we're eating pasta
(with pesto plus garlic)
when
the bell rings
and another one of us
shows up
eats the fettucine
talks about much maybe
it's love much
114   maybe
it's not exactly love but
anyhow
the pasta's hot/the wine
goes down
real easily and before you know
it
two bottles stand
side by side and we
head
for the beach in San Francisco
and loud on the car box
it's The Gypsy Kings
and Osa's in the back with binoculars
looking at the tail lights of the truck
in the right lane

(or the bridge lights
or the stars)
and we pass the binoculars around
like marijuana
but the visuals seem
better
so we're laughing as we roll
over the Big Bay
and speeding
while each one of us imagines what
romance would look like
through binoculars
(Binocular Romance)
which reminds me
I'm not sure

about the color of your eyes
then
we turn left to find
the Pacific Ocean
and the sand
and the almighty all night
full moon
that begins the end of a whole lot
and I'm thinking
where am I
where are you
and the ocean agitates
the slumber of my curiosity:
Cross currents
slash into the shallow surf
curls of these high tide waters

and the tides dissolve in dizzy
disarray
and how the soft air will accept the breathing
of my timid witness
warm
and restless in the dark
confinement of a moon
as radiant
as imperative
as this lyrical retrieval
of your smile
three thousand miles
away

I train my eyes to see
what I am suffering
not to touch

late afternoon and the air
dissolves to luminous and elongated
molecules
a heartfelt mercury as delicate
as compelling
as the melted movements
of your lips

This must be the longitudinal
anatomy of rain

this cosmic commotion twice
bestirred by the exact
infinitesimal
assertions of your body's
dance

These must be the subterranean
beginnings of all light

These shimmer surfaces
that glow arterial below the frosted rooftops
and the thick

surrender of the open
trusted
trees
And like the stars
above the dark far streets
between us
heat
develops into liquid
documents of fire
and there
and here
moving through these beautiful waters
you and I
become the river

I Must Become a Menace
to My Enemies
Dedicated to the Poet Agostinho Neto,
President of The People's Republic of Angola: 1976

I

I will no longer lightly walk behind
a one of you who fear me:
                              Be afraid.
I plan to give you reasons for your jumpy fits
and facial tics

I will not walk politely on the pavements
    anymore
and this is dedicated in particular
to those who hear my footsteps
or the insubstantial rattling of my grocery
cart
then turn around
see me
and hurry on
away from this impressive terror I must be:
I plan to blossom bloody on an afternoon
surrounded by my comrades singing
terrible revenge in merciless
accelerating
rhythms
But
I have watched a blind man studying his face.

I have set the table in the evening and sat down
to eat the news
Regularly
I have gone to sleep.
There is no one to forgive me.
The dead do not give a damn.
I live like a lover
who drops her dime into the phone
just as the subway shakes into the station
wasting her message
cancelling the question of her call:

fulminating or forgetful but late
and always after the fact that could save or

condemn me

I must become the action of my fate.

II

How many of my brothers and my sisters
will they kill
before I teach myself
retaliation?
Shall we pick a number?
South Africa for instance:
do we agree that more than ten thousand
in less than a year but that less than
five thousand slaughtered in more than six
months will
WHAT IS THE MATTER WITH ME?

I must become a menace to my enemies.

III

And if I
if I ever let you slide
who should be extirpated from my universe
who should be cauterized from earth
completely
(lawandorder jerkoffs of the first the
terrorist degree)
then let my body fail my soul
in its bedevilled lecheries

And if I
if I ever let love go
because the hatred and the whisperings
become a phantom dictate I o-
bey in lieu of impulse and realities
(the blossoming flamingos of my
wild mimosa trees)
then let love freeze me
out.

I must become
I must become a menace to my enemies.

Evidently Looking at the Moon Requires a Clean Place To Stand

The forest dwindling narrow and irregular
to darken out the starlight on the ground
where needle shadows
signify the moon a harsh
a horizontal blink that lays the land
implicit to the movement of your body
is
the moon

You'd think I was lying to you
if I described precisely
how
implicit to the feeling of your lips
are luminous announcements
of more mystery than Arizona
more than just the imperturbable
convictions
of the cow

Headfirst into a philosophy
and

so sexy
chewing up the grass

Roman Poem Number Five
For Millen and for Julius
and for Peter and for Eddie

I

This is a trip that strangers make
a journey ending on the beach where things
come together like four fingers on his
rather predictable
spine exposed by stars and
when he said this
has never happened before he
meant something
specific to himself because he could not
meet me anywhere inside but
you know
we were both out of the water
both out of it
and really what we wanted was
to screw ourselves into
the place

Pompeii
the Sarno River to the south
the mountain of Vesuvius to the north
the river did not burn
none of the records indicate
a burning river

of all that went before the earth
remembers nothing
                    everywhere you see
the fertility of its contempt
the sweet alyssum blooming
in the tomb
an inward town
well suited to the lives
unraveled and undone
despite the secretly coloring
interior of their sudden blasted
walls

Vensuvius created and destroyed

WHOLE TOP OF THE MOUNTAIN
BLOWN OFF
you can hum some words
catchy like the title of a song
(a little song)
WHOLE TOP OF THE MOUNTAIN
BLOWN OFF
                    (play it again sam)

Pompeii
the mountain truly coming to the men
who used to walk these streets these
sewer drains (the difference is
not very clear)

juniper and cypress trees
inspire the dark the only definite the trying
forms on the horizon sky and sea and the Bay
of Naples
single trees
against abstraction
trees

the mainstreet moves directly
to the mouth the mountaintop
a vicious puckering

This is a place where all the lives
are planted in the ground
the green things grow
the other ones
volcanic victims of an overflow
a fireflushing tremble
soul unseasonal
in rush and rapture
well they do not grow
they seed the rest of us
who prowl
with plundersucking polysyllables
to rape the corpse
to fuck the fallen down and died
long time ago
again.

his hands removes some of the sand on my neck
with difficulty

    did the river did the river burn

Pliny the Younger who delivered the volcano
who arrested the eruption into words
excited arrogant terrific
an exclusive
elegant account of mass destruction
79 A.D. that Johnny-on-the-spot say nothing
much about the river and
but eighteen is not too old to worry
for the rivers of the world

          around the apple flesh and fit
love holds easily
the hard skin soft enough

        picture him sweet but cold
        above the eyebrows
        just a teenage witness with his
        pencil
        writing down disaster

some say
put that apple into uniform
the tree itself wears buttons
in the spring

     VISITING DISASTER IS A WEIRD IDEA
     WHETHER YOU THINK ABOUT IT OR
     NOT

for example limestone the facade the statues the
limestone statues of the everyone of them dead and
dead and dead and no more face among the buried
under twenty-seven feet of limestone other various
in general all kinds of dust covering the dead the
finally comfortable statues of the dusty smell today
the nectar fragrance of the sun knocks down my
meter taking notes the wheel ruts gutter drains the
overhanging upperstories the timber superstructure
the dead the very dead the very very dead dead
farmland pasture dead potato chip dead rooms of
the dead the no longer turbulent blazing the no
longer glorious inglorious the finish of the lime-
stone building limestone statues look at the wild
morninglories red and yellow laughter at the dying
who dig into the death of limestone hard to believe
the guide leads people to the public baths I Bagni di
Publicci to talk about slaves and masters and how
many sat at table he explains the plumbing where
men bathed and where the women (bathed) hot
water cold where the wall has a hole in it or where
there is no hole in the wall and the tourists listening
and nobody asks him a question how about the
living and the dead how about that

Pompeii and we are people who notice the mosaic
decorations
of a coffin
we claim to be ordinary men and women or
extraordinary

elbows touching
cameras ready
sensible shoes
architects archaeologists classical
scholars one poet
Black and White and Jewish and Gentile and partly
   young
and married and once or twice married but
why do we follow
all
inquisitive
confessional or
necrophilomaniac or anyhow
alone

I am not here for you and I will stay there
we are disturbing the peace of the graveyard and
that is the believable limit of our impact
our intent
no
tonight he will hold me hard on the rocks of the
   ground
if the weather is warm and if
it doesn't rain

2

KEEP MOVING KEEP MOVING
the past is practically
behind us

half skull and teeth
knocked down running an

extreme tilt jerk tilted skull
stiff on its pole plaster cartilage
the legs apart like elbows
then the arms themselves the mouth
of the dead man tense defending still
the visitors peruse these plaster
memories of people
forms created in the cinders
living visitors admire the poise
of agony the poise of agony is
absolute
and who would call it sculpture
raise your own hand to the fire

IN THE VILLA DEI MISTERI
THERE ARE BLACK WALLS

another plaster person
crouched into his suffocation

yes well in the 14th century BC
they had this remarkable
bedroom where
they would keep one bed
or (some authorities say)
two beds
maybe it was the 15th

Pompeii
the unfamiliar plain
the unfamiliar guilt
annihilated men and women who
most likely
never heard of archaology of
dusty lust

all the possible homes were never built
   (repeat)

'What's that?'
'That's a whorehouse, honey.'

130 freckle hands chafing together
urbane
he tells the group that in
the declinium
women stayed apart with their loom
(in the declinium

occasional among the rocks the buttercups
obscure until the devil of the land)

Perhaps Aristotle said the size
of a city
should take a man's shout to ears
even on the edge
but size never took anything
much no matter what the porno
makes believe but

what will take in the
scream of a what will
take it in?

current calculations postulate the
human beings half the size of the market
place

BEES

LIZARDS

walls plus walls inhibit action on the lateral
or
with all them walls now how
you gone get next to me
                the falling of ashes
                the rolling lava

the way the things be happening
that garden story figleaf it belong
on top your head

                they had these industries these
                wool and fish sauce
                ways to spend the
                fooler

                even the moon is dark among us
                except for the lights by the mountainside
                except for the lights

20,000 people
subject
to Vesuvius in natural violence blew
up the handicrafted
fortress spirit of Pompeii
the liquid mangling
motley blood and lava
subject
20,000 people

KEEP MOVING KEEP MOVING

to them the theatre was 'indispensable'
seats for 5,000 fabulous acoustics
132 what
was the performance of the people
in surprise
the rhythm chorus speaking
rescue
multitudes to acrobat survival
one last action on that last
entire stage

today the cypress tree tips dally
wild above the bleachers

when it happened what is happening to us

to hell with this
look at the vegetables blue
in the moonlight

                    a pinetree colonnade
                    the wall just under
                    and the one man made

come to Pompeii
touch my tongue with yours
study the cold formulation of a fearful fix
grid patterns to the streets
the boundaries 'unalterable'

the rights of property in stone
the trapezoidal plot the signals
of possession

                    laughter
                    (let's hear it loud)
                    the laughing of the lava   **133**
                    tell me
                    stern
                    rigid
                    corpulent
                    stories

the mountains surround the wastebasket bricks of our
    inquiry
in part
the waters barely stir with poison or with fish

                    I think I know
                    the people who
                    were here
                    where I am

3

my love completely and
one evening anywhere
I will arrive
the right way
given
up to you
and keep no peace

my body sings the force
of your disturbing legs

                    WHAT DID YOU SAY?
                    NO THANKS.
                    WHAT DID YOU SAY?

Vesuvius
when Daddy Adam did what he did
the blame the bliss beginning
of no thanks
this is a bad connection
are you serious?

        the river did not burn

the group goes on
among the bones we travel
light into a new
starvation
            Pompeii was yesterday

here is Herculaneum
a second interesting testimony
to excuse me but how
will you try to give testimony
to a mountain?

there it is baby there it is
FURTHER EXCAVATION INTO
HERCULANEUM
ARRESTED TODAY BY RESSINI living
inhabitants impoverished the non-
descript Ressini town on top the
ruins of

amazing Herculaneum
constructed on an earlier rehearsal flow
of lava maybe
courage or like that a seashore
a resort the remnant spread the
houses under houses
tall trees underlying grass the
pine and palm trees spring toward
Ressini grass retaining walls against the water
where there is no water and the sound of children
crying from which city is it Ressisni is it
Herculaneum that
does not matter does it is it
the living or the visited the living or
the honored ercolano

SUCK
SUCK HARD

'Here's where they sold spaghetti'
the leafy sound the feel
of the floor the tile
the painting of a wineglass
a wineglass on the wall unprecedented
turquoise colors would
the red walls make you warm
in winter

INFORMATION

WAS

NOT AVAILABLE

THE POOR

OF RESSINI

REFUSE

TO COOPERATE

WITH AUTHORITIES

you better watch out
next summer
and Ressini gone slide

down inside them fancy
stones
and stay there
using
flashlight
or whatever

NOBODY BUDGE
KEEP MOVING KEEP MOVING

cabbages cauliflower broccoli
the luminous leaves on the land

4

yesterday and yesterday
Paestum dates from four
hundred fifty years before the Christ
a fertile lowland calmly naked
and the sky excites the rubble flowers
in between
the mountains and the water
bleaching gentle
in the Middle Ages
mountainstreams came down
and made the meadow into marsh
marble travertine deposits when
the mountains left the land
the memory
deranged the water
turned the plants
to stone

this is the truth the people left this place alone

we are somewhere wounded by the wind
a mystery
a stand deserted by the trees

drizzling rain
destroys the dandelion
and your lips enlarge the glittering
of silence

        Paestum dedicated temples dedicated
        to the terra cotta figurines of trust
        the women in becoming mother of the world
        the midwives hold her arms
        like wings

the river does not burn

        delivering the life

the temple does not stand

still

        PERMISSION GRANTED TO PRESENT
        STONE SEX THE ECSTASY OF
        PAESTUM

4 main rows of
six in front
the tapering the girth the groove
the massive lifted fit of things
the penis worshiping
fecundity
fecundity
the crepis

stylobate
the cella
columns in entasis
magic
diminution
Doric
flutes
entablature
the leaning
curvilinear
the curve
the profile
magic
elasticity
diameter

effacement

THE TEMPLE IS THE COLOR OF A LIFE
ON STONE THE SUN CONTINUES
BLISTERING THE SURFACE
TENDERLY

WHAT TIME IS IT?

as we approach each other
someone else is making
a movie
there are horses
one or two beautiful men
and
birds flying
away

These poems
they are things that I do
in the dark
reaching for you
whoever you are
and are you ready?

These words
they are stones in the water
running away

140 *These skeletal lines*
They are desperate arms for my longing and love.

I am a stranger
learning to worship the strangers
around me

whoever you are
whoever I may become.